The Blight Better Off Dead

by

Nicholas Scott

LETTER 26

productions

The blood was almost dry, though the dawning light still winked off of it. A coppery scent stained the air, pluming thick above the ravaged corpse. I fought an urge to vomit, retching involuntarily, but there was nothing to purge but the acidic bile burning my throat.

I looked back at Jimmy. How he was able to sleep mystified me. But there he was sleeping like a baby, his hands tucked under his head for a makeshift pillow and the dirty ratty blanket covered him to the waist. He had his back against the wall farthest away from the door.

He didn't love me. I knew that now. It wasn't like there were many other choices left for us. After The Blight, we found each other. Truth be told when we first encountered him, I was sorely tempted to behead the fucker just to be safe. But he had food, and a big sword he called Swinging Dick, which he swung with great bravado, and a smiling charm that won my sister over almost immediately.

As if he felt me looking at him, Jimmy stirred. I saw the pink bandanna wrapped around his wrist. It was Ashley's.

After a month of close calls and deadly encounters his heroics were too much for Ash to ignore. Jimmy was her knight in shining armor. One day she was watching him, cautiously keeping her distance, the next she was walking side by side with him, bumping casually against him. Then she was holding his hands. The first time I saw them kissing; secretly, in an orange grove, under a thick canopy, with so many oranges dotting the ground around them, I knew *I* had fallen for him too.

Ash was dead now and all we had, Jimmy and I, was each other.

The breaking glass brought me out of my reverie. I turned quickly, peering past the shadows that striped the floor inside the burned out house with bands of bright moonlight. I nearly jumped when Jimmy came up behind me. Heat flowed from his body and enveloped me and I could smell him. He was dirty, we were both dirty, filthy wouldn't be an exaggeration, but the scent of him, his earthy musk calmed me instantly.

"Good morning." His breath tickled my neck and I fought from shivering. I imagined his lips on me, an easy enough thing to imagine. After Ash he turned to me.

He had done everything he could to keep her safe, everything except save her. He killed four of them. They came ambling out of the night. The fire drew them. I had warned them, but Ash wanted a romantic fire and fresh cooked rabbit.

For my part, I left them alone. That was something I carried with me. Leaving them alone, to their groping and kissing, turning a deaf ear to the panting and moaning. I'd heard far too much of it. The first time, I pleasured myself to the sounds of it, imagining myself in her place, feeling his hands, on me, the taste of his mouth, and the weight of his body atop me. It left me feeling torn and hollow.

Ash, for her part, knew of my predicament.

We were only two years into The Blight. We'd be seniors now, she and I, or just graduated. It was late summer I think. Technology was non-existent, well, it existed but without electricity, what good was it? We had stumbled upon a cache of batteries at an abandoned Walmart, apparently overlooked by the looters and the scavengers after them. Even better, was the case of wireless portable chargers. After two years of silence, without radio or television or iPhone, I listened to my playlist in wonder, reliving those first times in an almost euphoric high.

We should have thrown them out, the chargers, though the notion itself is ridiculous. On more than one occasion they'd been more trouble that they were worth. We fought over them, using them too much, rationing how long we used them, what we used them for.

We found a world band radio in the basement of an abandoned house. Every day starting at 2:00 and then in two-hour increments until 10:00, we'd turn on the radio on and listen for 10 minutes. An occasional burst of static, an automated emergency signal and once a man whose ravings frightened us more than anything else, was all we heard. We'd gone through 20 of the 24 chargers. Sixteen wasted on the radio, the other four charged a wistful musical melancholy that lay on us like clouds as we listened to a Billboards top 100 from 2014.

Jimmy blamed me for Ash's death. He was with her, which was why I took a charger and my iPhone and climbed one of the grander trees that towered into the night sky. I climbed high enough, the canopy hiding all but a few glimmers of amber light from the fire they had built. I stared up at the sky; the stars almost seemed to glisten in concert with the music, a miserable light show with Great Big World and Christina tearing at my soul.

I glanced down once and they were in each other's embrace.

I had climbed high enough to be away, but not high enough where I couldn't see them. The firelight glowed off of his back; I could just make out the exquisite musculature, his arms taut as he held himself up off of her. I could see Ash's head thrown back, her mouth open in a climactic O, her nails digging into his flesh.

They came, ambling but fast.

The Blight was something out of a Stephen King novel. Not a government mistake bringing the world to the brink of complete destruction, but a terrorist attack. The virus itself was manufactured in a sterile lab somewhere buried deep in the Pamir Mountains of Afghanistan. The attack was a vial smashed on the floor of Grand Central Station. Within a month, 80% of the world's population, over 5 billion people, was dead.

I looked back at Jimmy. The kiss on my neck caught me by surprise, then he pulled me back into the shadows as he took Swinging Dick and stood sentry. "Go to sleep. I'll wake you when it's time to go."

#

"Wake up." Jimmy looked tired. The dark circles under his eyes were but the most obvious sign of his fatigue but his stride back to the brightening window proved his exhaustion all the more. I stretched feeling my own fatigue. I crawled out of the makeshift bed and rolled up the blanket. It smelled like Jimmy, and while he looked out the window, I lifted it to take in his scent. It was comforting; I could practically feel the oxytocin surging through my body.

We didn't talk and he worked fast at prying the boards off the remnants of the bedroom door. He drew the door open with a cautious hesitation. The rest of the house was quiet and dark, the air stagnant. We stood on the landing.

The corpse jerked spasmodically, its hand grasping blindly at nothing. I didn't think it sensed us. Jimmy had nearly decapitated it on our last ditch dash up the stairs. It was on the landing. I jerked when it reached out and grabbed my jacket. Jimmy, in a one-two stroke hacked off its arm and then it's head.

Nothing stirred below us. We stood stock still, listening. That was the easiest way to know if they were there.

The virus was highly contagious and lethal, its primary symptom: severe necrosis and organ degeneration due to a hemotoxic enzyme; bloody bilious eruptions were not uncommon. After the virus ran its course, like a raging fire through a drought stricken forest, the first signs of The Blight began to appear. Normal apparently healthy individuals, spared the ravages of the initial viral outbreak, began attacking each other, their dispositions suddenly rabid, their nature base and animalistic. They were reduced to guttural mewling cannibals. The mewling was incessant.

"Do you hear anything?" Jimmy held his sword, his knuckles white.

I shook my head and took a cautious step. The floor under us creaked but the rest of the house remained quiet. Then, my stomach growled, almost as loudly as the floorboards and I couldn't help but grin.

I watched Jimmy digging through the pockets of his coat. He pulled out a fun-sized Snickers candy bar. He held it out to me and continued walking, not looking back.

I wondered how many more he had left.

#

Ashley and I drove north up 35 until the roads were impassible, then we hiked. The interstate was a motor graveyard. The dead were ubiquitous. The almost dead, the blighted, were not so numerous,

We crossed paths with Jimmy at a Circle K in Ardmore Oklahoma. The burned out remnants of a Motel 6, its swimming pool filled with beer cans and from the smell of it, a great deal of urine, was the scenic backdrop. Jimmy was perched on the roof below the blue sign with the big red six.

Ash and I were almost feral by that point, hungry beyond description and reduced to our own sort of monosyllabic communication. The fact that we weren't at each other's throats was the only indication that we weren't blighted ourselves.

"Hey!" His voice echoed in the silence like a shotgun. Ash jumped and latched on to me tightly and we ran and ducked behind one of the Circle K's gas pumps. "I see you."

He sounded almost cheerful in this horrific landscape where we found ourselves. The sun was close to setting, it burned almost red and striated clouds, also red, slashed the sky.

"What do you want?"

I tried finding the source of the voice, Ash's grip around me constricting. I saw the flash of a lighter and thought I could even smell that first scent of burning tobacco as he lit a cigarette.

"Nothing." I called back. "Nothing." I reiterated. "We're just passing through. We don't want any trouble. "

I heard him scrabbling down the roof, saw the telltale glow of his cigarette. He walked with a swagger and carried a sword, the blade flat on his shoulder.

10

"You don't want to go up that way. There's a lot of *them* up there." He gestured with the point of his sword. "Its almost dark. Stay with me. *Mi casa es su casa.*"

I could just make out his grin, his eyes sparkling as he eyed Ash. I stepped over in front of her, blocking his view. Then blushed as he eyed me with an equal interest.

"Come on. Y'all look hungry."

Instead of walking back to the Motel 6, he headed towards the Circle K. The windows and doors were boarded up and in front of the actual pane glass, what glass remained, that is, both a security gate and bars. One of the bigger windows had been broken, the shattered glass glistening in the sunset like burnished rubies. It looked like someone had tried, unsuccessful, to pull the bars down with a car and a chain. A chained snaked half way across the sidewalk from the bars to a rusted out bumper.

Jimmy pulled a clump of keys from his pocket and selected one. The gate lifted easily, but with a grating rattle. He pulled it back down behind us after unlocking the barred door. *Jimmy's Place* was spray painted in neon orange.

"Welcome to *mi casa.*"

I watched him warily, though he seemed quite at ease in our presence. Of course he didn't let go of the sword, which glimmered in what little reflected light remained of the sunset. He hopped up on the counter and nodded towards a hoard of canned food.

"How long have you been here?" I asked for conversation's sake, attacking a can of Chef Boyardee with a hand-crank can opener.

He shrugged, staring off at nothing. "Forever."

"All by yourself?" I watched him; the light in his eyes, the bravado, the swagger, all of it gone, like a mirage, heat waves in the distance.

"Except for *them*." He nodded. "Nobody normal till I saw you two, for a long time."

I heard Ashley laugh and turned, watching as she ripped open a box of Twinkies. I couldn't remember the last time I heard her laugh.

#

We were clear of the house and back on the highway before the sun broke the horizon.

"I'm sorry, you know." Jimmy didn't look at me as we trudged our way north, weaving between the abandoned cars and debris that littered the interstate. We'd decided the best way to find more food was to scavenge for it in the vehicles along the motorway.

Jimmy was a pro when it came to scavenging; he had pretty much scavenged everything within a 10-mile radius of the Circle K. His stockpile would have lasted us years, had we stayed there. His collection of guns was remarkable, but he had an affinity for blades too.

I didn't say anything.

"She was my mother." His voice was pained beyond description.

Ash and I lost our parents years before the initial viral attack and The Blight. Sometimes I couldn't remember what they looked like so the idea of holding on to them as long as possible was understandable.

#

The noise woke me; foot steps on broken glass. I darted to consciousness immediately and stared into the dark. A dawning light glowed over the tops of the boards that covered the windows and a tiny breeze fluttered cobwebs in the corner of the Circle K. I watched the gossamer webs dance on the breeze, all the while listening. Another step crunched from outside. The mewling cry got my heart racing and I was on the verge of hyperventilating I was breathing so hard.

I looked over at Jimmy. He lay perfectly still, but his eyes were open and reflected a silver patina of light.

"They can't get in, you know." Jimmy rolled onto his back and lit a cigarette. "They try sometimes, but it's too complicated. Their brains are too simple now, pretty much mush, or Swiss cheese." I could hear his cigarette in the quiet as he inhaled. "My mom said it was like the virus ate only certain parts of the brain. She was a nurse before."

I sat up, crisscross applesauce and looked down at Ash to make sure I didn't wake her. Jimmy looked over at her too.

"You two twins?"

I nodded. I was the older one, by four minutes. When we were asked, and we always were, even though it was blatantly obvious that we were twins, Ash would often say it was the most peaceful four minutes of her life. I would stick my tongue out at her and tell her she missed me and she knew it.

"She's pretty." Jimmy observed.

I nodded. We were pretty much identical, but she was prettier. At least in my eyes. And guys aren't pretty anyways. So naturally, Ash was prettier.

I heard the chain on the sidewalk outside rattle and looked over quickly.

"It's fine." Jimmy reassured me. He sat up, his eyes darting to the glass cases of the walk-in cooler

The Circle K had a back up generator and apparently enough gasoline to run the thing for quite sometime. The hum of the generator and that of the refrigeration unit reminded me of the fan that I kept by my bed growing up, the noise a distraction that more times than not lulled me to sleep.

"There's milk. It's powdered, but I made it yesterday, so it should be nice and cold, now."

I hadn't had milk in ages; it seemed, a lifetime. I'd never had powdered milk before but milk was milk.

"And there's cereal."

There was too. He had cases of those little boxes of cereal, the ones they gave you in elementary school for breakfast. He had a variety to choose from, but it was obvious he preferred Fruit Loops; the garbage can in the corner was filled with empty little red Fruit Loop boxes, Toucan Sam smiling maniacally.

I could hear nails on wood, as if the thing outside was trying to claw its way through to us, but Jimmy still seemed relaxed.

"I don't mind sharing." Jimmy hopped up and ambled over to a coffee station, the chrome fixture had lost its brilliant luster, but was neat and tidy. There was an opened package of Styrofoam bowls and a little silverware caddy filled with plastic ware. He flipped a switch on the coffee machine and the little power button glowed brilliantly.

"You have coffee?" I sighed the question more than actually asked it. One of the things I missed most in the entire world was my Starbucks. No more Frappuccino or macchiato or vanilla blond roast.

Jimmy opened the cabinet and pulled out a gallon of purified water and poured it in the coffee maker. I watched him with rapt attention as he opened the coffee and my heart leapt at the scent of it. He filled a filter and set the machine to its task.

"Seriously. Inside the walk-in. There's milk on the

14

left hand side. Past the Dr Pepper, which is mine by the way, you can have anything else in there, but the Dr Pepper is mine." He indicated the big metallic door with his head. "Could you get it for me? I like milk in my coffee."

"Sure." I glanced over at Ash. She still slept, though she had rolled onto her side and was facing the cigarette display. Most of the cigarettes were gone, especially the Marlboros. The no name brands down at the bottom of the display were still almost full.

The metal handle of the walk in refrigerator was cold. I tugged on it and felt a delightful plume of cold air gush past me. It was cool and sweet and inviting, but no light came on. I pulled the door completely open and while my eyes had adjusted to the darkness of the Circle K, it was almost pitch black in the walk-in and I couldn't see anything beyond the ashy gray halo of light.

"In the back, to the left. There's a clear path. Nothing to trip over." He called out. "You're not scared of a little dark are you?" He chided.

"No." My voice held no conviction as I stepped into the cooler.

The door slammed closed behind me and I yelled with a start. I rushed back to the door. It was solid and I pounded on it and tried to slam it open with my body. I pushed on the emergency plunger, that in my minds eye saw as a brilliant red, but in the complete and utter darkness, I couldn't tell.

I tired of pounding and slid down the door.

"I'm sorry." The words were muted and coming from the other side of the door.

It was then I heard the mewling coming from the dark in the back of the cooler.

Wide-awake and buzzing with adrenaline, my senses in overdrive, I listened. The mewling echoed up from the back of the walk-in but I could hear no telltale ambulatory drag. But I wasn't taking any chances. Along my left hand side were empty aluminum racks in front of the glass case doors. I stepped into the darkness, three great strides was all I was willing to take, and jerked the farthest rack in front of me away from the glass doors and knocked it to the floor. As I walked backwards I knocked another and then a third to create a makeshift barricade between it and me. A gray halo of light emanated faintly through the case doors, but too faint to show me where it was. I jerk another rack down for good measure.

With the commotion, the mewling increased in volume. Another sound; sandpaper on cement, forced me into overdrive. It was coming. I reached blindly in the dark for anything I could use as a weapon. Something furry sent me scrambling backwards against the walk-in door. I pounded on it again; pushing the emergency release in hopes that maybe I could get out. But it caught quickly.

A metallic screech echoed up from the back. It had reached the barricade, pulling at the first rack.

I went back to my search for weapons. I reached to the right, into the darkness. I felt the chill of cold metal: round canisters with tubes running up and into the wall.

Next to the coffee station was a carbonated drinks station. These must be the CO_2 canisters. I remembered changing them out at the movie theatre I had worked at when I was in high school. I hefted one and it rocked easily. I grabbed the end of the hose and started turning the nozzle. Air hissed louder and louder the more I turned. I found the handle and closed off the valve then finished removing the nozzle.

One of the metal racks tumbled loudly in front of me.   The hungry cry was closer; too close as far as I was concerned.   I heaved the canister off the cement floor, raising it over my head.   It was heavier than I thought and I leaned back forcefully against the door, the canister clanging.   I listened for it and then flung the canister with as much strength as I could muster.

The canister rang like a bell when it hit the cement floor. It bounced once then again before it rolled to a stop. The thing was still coming.   I reached over quickly and tried working the nozzle off the second canister.   I could hear a shriek of metal on cement as it struggled against the barrier.   I wrestled with the nozzle but it was too tight.   I was crying, both tears and a litany of curse words as I jerked on the hose trying to rip it free of the canister.

Another rack scraped across the cement.   I grabbed the hose with both hands and closed my eyes and jerked as hard as I could, pulling it out from the wall.   I heard a muted thump from outside the walk-in.   I pulled again, bracing one foot against the wall itself growling as I pulled a tug-of-war with the soda machine on the other side of the wall. I didn't think it would come free until I was tumbling backwards.   I landed on my ass painfully, throwing my hand backwards, It sank into another furry squishy *something.*   I fought the urge to vomit fought the images of what it might be. I wiped my hands frantically on the floor and then on my pant legs then scrambled back up to my feet.

It felt like the thing was right next to me.   I turned towards the back of the walk-in and pulled the hose like a rope until I had the end up it then looped it quickly in a ball.   The last thing I needed was to fling the canister and have the hose wrapped around me and it falling short of its target.   I grabbed up the canister.

The morning light was brighter through the glass case door. I could see movement in the gray darkness beyond me and inside the walk-in. I lifted the canister; it was heavier than the first one. I flung it. I thought the trajectory was low but heard a liquid thud and the mewling cut off sharply. I tried to peer into the gray darkness. I listened, holding my breath. I could hear my heart pounding, from exertion, adrenaline and fear. But I couldn't hear it. I slid down the door coming to rest on my ass.

I sat, for I don't know how long, I think I might have even fallen asleep for a bit until a beam of light cut through the darkness from outside the glass case. I heard Ash's voice, muted but frantically calling. The beam of light caught me in the face and I shaded my eyes, squinting against the sudden brightness. The light zigzagged back and forth as she ran towards the walk-in door. I heard her jerking on the door handle, could actually see the emergency plunger pulling into the door mechanism. There was faint and muffled banging and then finally the door opened.

Ash stood in the doorway, in one hand Jimmy's long sword and the flashlight glowed brilliantly in the other. I took the flashlight from her and aimed it into the darkness.

I stepped lightly towards it. The canister had landed on her head crushing it quickly against the metal support bar. She must have been trying to climb over it.

I shot the beam down to the floor into the corner. The furry mess grinned; hair and flesh slagging off a grimacing skull. The throat and shoulder had been bitten and chunks of flesh torn from the body. A thick dense furry mold had grown over the rest of the corpse. I turned quickly and vomited into the corner.

#

"You know what, you can go fuck yourself." I shook my head.

"She was my moth…." Jimmy tried to respond.

You tried to *feed* me to her, fucker!" The memory was still too fresh. Even after everything else. Even after what happened to Ash.

"How many?" I had stopped walking and was leaning on a old rusty Ford Econoline van, the windows busted out and I heard flies buzzing inside, a sound that had become increasingly familiar. I didn't dare look to see what they were feasting on.

"What?" Jimmy had stopped too, though he didn't turn to look at me.

"How many others did you kill?"

I didn't kill any…"

"No you're right. They went in to get the milk and just didn't come back out: a little tea party in the walk-in cooler."

"She was…."

"I don't give a shit who she was."

I didn't know why I was bringing this up now. It had been months; back in Ardmore. I hadn't forgiven him but too much had happened since; it seemed stupid to hold it against him now.

Ash had died outside of Wichita, two weeks later.

Now, Jimmy and I just crossed over the city limits of Kansas City. Route 66 had nothing on post Blight Interstate 35. I wondered where all these people had been going. Abandoned vehicles stretched as far as the eye could see in both directions; an eternal traffic jam.

Packs of feral dogs darted and weaved under and around the vehicles, watching warily, dashing off as we approached. Trees encroached upon the blacktop and broke through the asphalt in places. A bridge over the Arkansas River was a veritable hanging garden, thick vines growing the length of the stay cables to the top of the towers. Ash would have really liked it.

#

When I first saw the sign for Wichita, I thought maybe we had gotten turned around and were headed in the wrong direction.

"You're thinking Wichita Falls, stupid." Ash pointed out. She was holding Jimmy's hand and they were walking together; young lovers without a care in the world.

I stuck my tongue out at her and she smiled back at me then turned away.

I was a little offended that she'd so easily forgotten everything that had happened at the Circle K. But then again, Jimmy's charisma was difficult to ignore. I'd found myself drawn to him just as Ash had.

He was attractive with his dirty blond hair and blue eyes; he was taller than me, and having hoarded plenty of food at the Circle K, he hadn't lost much in the way of body mass. He was quick to smile and that smile was disarming and charming. To look at him, you'd never know there was anything wrong with the world. That, in and of itself, was attractive enough, but he made us laugh too.

"We should find a place to camp." Jimmy looked back at me and winked. My gut fluttered and I chided myself for letting him get to me. I think he knew it too as he played it up, grabbing Ash's ass as they walked. She squealed and slapped at his hand only to pull it around her waist, pulling him against her.

I could only sigh, denying my frustration and desire. I looked away.

He pulled a Radio Flyer all-terrain wagon; two large oversized milk crates carried foodstuff and a cache of handguns and bullets.

Big black scavenger birds drifted in lazy circles above us, biding their time, in a dirty sky painted dusty orange. We had just crossed over the Arkansas River again and were making our way through what remained of a city park. It appeared as though a fire had ravaged a great deal of it, only recently. However, a large copse of trees stood silhouetted against the dark city skyline. Fields of natural turf grew with wild abandon, devouring any and all semblance of their prior manicured state.

The copse of trees were poplars; cottonwoods, most of them, skeletal, their branches gnarled but grabbing at the sky. A few however had escaped the fire and were lush and vibrant sending seeds aplenty afloat in cottony drifts on the breeze. My eyes travelled up the great trunk of one of the trees and I marked my spot, a thick sturdy branch for my post. I headed straight for the tree.

I've always had an affinity for trees. When I was little I would spend hours upon hours climbing as high as I could in any tree that could support my weight. When visiting my grandparents near Weatherford, I found the peach trees to be an aromatic sanctuary. I'd fall asleep under them, counting the fruit.

"I want a fire." Ash acted like we were on a camping trip.

I looked over at her, shaking my head.

"Just a small one. For a little bit." She continued, not looking at me but at Jimmy instead.

"It's not a good idea." I said it in a sing-songy voice because I knew she wasn't going to listen to me. I hoped Jimmy would.

"It'll be fine." Jimmy draped an arm over Ash's shoulder and pulled her closer, giving her a quick kiss. My glare went unobserved. "Besides everything's already burned down."

"That's not why it's a bad idea."

The virus struck major metropolitan areas hardest and the blighted were ubiquitous afterwards. Graphic scenes of military forces putting down hoards were numerous early on; before there were more blighted than normal folks and there was an actual audience for television.

"Wichita is too big. Too many people, too many of *them.*" Just saying it, I couldn't help but scan the horizon. It was still daylight. They tended to avoid daylight, but occasionally one would stagger out blindly, mewling and hungry.

Jimmy had dispatched three of them since our leaving the Circle K, wielding his sword deftly; humanely, making quick work of the task.   Each time, afterwards, he'd clean the blade with a gravity that weighed his spirit. It was a merciful thing he did, but I wondered if he thought of his mother. He had kept her alive, in essence, a caged animal, unable to show her the same mercy.

Now he used his sword to hack at a tree.

#

Jimmy shot the rabbits while Ash started a fire. I watched him skin the rabbits with a calm efficiency, then he jam a long sharpened stick through the carcass; a makeshift spit, Our stomachs rumbled in concert as the meat roasted over the fire. My dad had told me once he had eaten rabbit when he was little but the idea was a little sad. They were so cute. Needless to say I had no qualms about it now.

Ash and Jimmy sat by the fire, their play growing more intimate until I had to leave. I grabbed one of the few remaining wireless chargers for the music that would drown them out. The music worked for a while, but there was a desolation to it that forced me to turn it off. I wound the ear buds around my phone and crammed it in my pocket.

Ash's campfire had burned itself out and both Jimmy and Ash were together under that ratty blanket that smelled of sex, even before he hooked up with my sister. She had complained at first, and he had thrown it over her and they both laughed when he crawled under after her. I couldn't help but wonder if that was what he smelled like once you got past the sword and his clothes; earthy and sweet.

The stars were innumerable, crushed diamonds on burnished velvet and the moon glowed so bright that the tree and I threw shadows.

I could see a night owl swooping through the darkness, hear its wings flapping and I thought I could hear the tiny shrieks of its prey before powerful talons tore into flesh and squeezed the life from it.

I could hear them talking too, Jimmy and Ash. Their voice carried on the wind. I couldn't make out the words but could tell the conversation was an intimate one.

Her hushed laughter made me glance over and that's when I noticed.

I didn't see them coming and I should have. I was high enough in the tree, I could see to the silvery moonlit river.

The first one was just a kid, but he was almost on top of them, before I saw him. I shouted as loud as I could and lunged down from one large branch to the next, then finally swinging my legs down I landed firmly on the ground.

Jimmy was already up and held his sword at the ready.

I ran as fast as I could, warning. "Behind you!"

Jimmy didn't look back; instead he swung his sword in a wide arc that nearly cut the boy in half. There was no pained cry, no wailing agony yearning for lost life, only a muted thump as it collapsed like a felled tree.

I ran to the little red wagon and dug through the milk crates, searching for and grabbing the first gun I saw, then slammed home one of the loaded clips.

I wasn't familiar with guns, so Jimmy had laid them all out, picking the ones he liked best, the ones that were easiest to handle; even for Ashley, and the ones that carried the most rounds. Then he showed us how to load them, aim them and fire them.

There was no hesitation as he draped his arms around me to show me how to aim. "Like this." He was warm; his breath, his hands, his finger over mine as he forced the trigger back. The cacophonous report and the jolt of the gun sent me against him with a startled laugh.

My first shot, at a real target, for my life, went wide and the gun jerked wildly and did nothing but bring more attention to me. I stopped and steadied my aim, held the gun firmly, listening to the hushed whisper in my head.

Like this. I watched it fall backwards, the bullet ripping out its throat.

Ash was a heavy sleeper and probably could have slept through the whole thing. But I woke her with a swift kick and she sat up quickly, her eyes round with fear. I gestured for her to be quiet and to stay put but then had to shoot over her shoulder at another of the dark figures staggering from the darkness. She scrambled to her feet, screaming, and then rushed over to Jimmy who nearly struck her with his sword only to stay his swing at the last moment.

One of the blighted strode through the ashy remnants of the fire; unfazed by the brightly lit coals it scattered. It fell upon Jimmy's blanket, clawing at it, snuffing at it like an animal and then tried biting through it. Finally it rose back up and looked around, smelling at the air. It must have caught my scent as it ambled a few steps in my direction. I shot it several times. Again there was no reaction, no expression of pain; it was just dead. It felt like a video game.

I looked around, trying to find Ash but didn't find her. Jimmy stood alone, looking too, jumping at sounds, his sword trembling. Three corpses lay around him, one of them twitching.

"Where is she?" I called out.

"She was just here!" He pivoted in a half circle, looking left and then right, then did a complete 360, peering into the darkness and calling out. "Ashley!"

I ran back to the little red wagon and dug around until I found the flashlight. The same one Ash had used when letting me out of the walk-in cooler.

Her scream chilled me. Jimmy and I ran full into the darkness, the flashlight's beam, a sword cutting a bright swath through the darkness.

25

A final shriek was cut short. Jimmy was in front of me as we ran, but when he heard her cry he stopped dead in his tracks. He sword arm dropped with his shoulders in resignation but I ran past him.

"Ash!"

She could have jumped into the river and probably saved herself. Instead she had stopped at the water's edge. The beam of light distracted it, but too late. It chewed at her throat, pausing a moment to look at me, growling. I turned off the flashlight and raised the pistol and emptied the clip. The last thing I remember was a splash as it fell into the river.

\#

"Where is she?"

It was obvious Jimmy had not slept and my question drained what little vitality remained in him. He slumped against the tree, his shirt riding up and exposing his stomach.

"She's gone."

"I know." I can't describe what I was feeling. The loss was too tremendous for words; part of me was gone.   "Where is she?"

Jimmy glanced over his shoulder, to the river and I followed with my own eyes. It seemed impossible that she had run that far, that we had run that far after her. Trees lined the river, tall thin poplars equidistant apart, planted as a decorative windbreak.   Glancing back I noticed the absence of corpses around the camp.

"They're all in the river."

I could see it now. The telltale drag lines stretching 300 yards at least.

"You put her in the river?"

"I had to." He was angry.

I nodded, though I didn't know why.

He looked at me and I could see the accusation.

"What?"

"She was still alive. All night long with that dead thing on top of her."

"No." I shook my head. "I heard it fall into the water."

"There were two."

I continued shaking my head. "I heard it fall…"

"There were two and…" He stopped, swallowing his words.

"And what?"

"I couldn't save her."

I wanted to yell at him. They had to have that stupid fire. She was dead because of it. "You killed her."

"I had to!" His voice cracked and tears lit his eyes in the morning light.

"What?"

He gripped the hilt of his sword then stood and flung it; winding once, twice and a third time before releasing it. I noted the blood on the blade and the realization rocked me. I watched the sword sail through the air, watched it fall to earth, watched it bounce once and then again before settling in the dirt and dust.

"I had to." His words came out in a sigh

#

Kansas City shined bright with the setting sun. Though the electricity was essentially dead, bright white lights shined here and there atop the skyline; the beacons.

After what happened to Ash, Jimmy had taken to listening to the world-band, insistent, obsessive. The first time he heard voices; he acted like it was nothing and dialed past it. He stared off as I gently took the radio. I dialed back, but found nothing but static. I looked at my watch, but the battery had long since died. I looked at the sun in the sky. And contemplated the time. For the next five days we heard nothing and I was beginning to think I had imagined it. We had two batteries left. When I heard the voices again, I listened with wonder, listening intently. Was this what it was like with the advent of the radio, the mystery of it, the novelty.

We had never used the radio to call out, assuming that it would use more power to broadcast that to receive. I spoke tentatively into the mike.

"Hello? Can you hear me?"

Static.

"Hello? Can you hear me?" I sat up straighter, listening with bated breath.

"This is Kansas City. We hear you. How many are you?"

I looked at Jimmy. He stared oblivious.

"Two. Just two."

~END~